M OF THE SOUTHERN DOWNPOURS

ALTON MELVAR M. DAPANAS (they/them), essayist, poet, and translator from the southern Philippines, is the author of *In the Name of the Body: Lyric Essays* (Canada: Wrong Publishing, 2023) and *Towards a Theory on City Boys: Prose Poems* (UK: Newcomer Press, 2021). Their works—published from South Africa to Japan, France to Australia, and translated into Chinese and Swedish—have appeared in *World Literature Today*, BBC Radio 4, *The White Review*, Sant Jordi Festival of Books, and the anthologies *Infinite Constellations* (University of Alabama Press) and *He, She, They, Us: Queer Poems* (Pan Macmillan UK). They currently serve as editor-at-large at *Asymptote*, and as assistant nonfiction editor at *Panorama: The Journal of Travel, Place, and Nature* and *Atlas & Alice Literary Magazine*. Formerly with *Creative Nonfiction* magazine, they've been nominated to *The Best Literary Translations* and twice to the Pushcart Prize for their lyric essays.

Find more at https://linktr.ee/samdapanas.

M of the
Southern Downpours

ALTON MELVAR M. DAPANAS

Downingfield Press

Cover design by Sofija Popovska, used under licence.
Author photo by Stefani J. Alvarez,
Book design by M. G. Mader.

ISBN 978-1-7635569-2-8 (paperback)

First published August 2024 by

Downingfield Press Proprietary Limited
Suite 346 / 585 Little Collins Street
Melbourne Victoria 3000
Australia

For a full list of addresses and contact information, visit
global.downingfield.com

Downingfield Press undertakes its work on the unceded lands of the Wurundjeri people of the Kulin Nation and pays respect to Elders past, present, and emerging.

A catalogue record for this work is available from the National Library of Australia

'POETRY BEYOND VERSE': RUMINATIONS ON THE PROSE POEM

after Solmaz Sharif's essay "The Near Transitive Properties of the Political and Poetical: Erasure"

On Facebook, a Filipino writer from generations before me—let's call her Madam M—would post, "If the idea you wish to convey is a little more complicated than [sic] can be contained in a statement, then write an essay," on she went, "only when your ideas are wrapped up in emotions … when you're lovestruck or lovelorn, should you write a poem." Smells like 1960s American New Criticism transplanted to the Philippines by Filipino writer-graduates of the Iowa Writers Workshop. One of these Iowa graduates, Edith L. Tiempo[1], a National Artist for Literature, would write, "with free verse as the poetic verbalizing today, it seems we are otherwise left with no inherent factors distinguishing between what is poetry and prose preening as poetry—and the nightmare apprehension that with no clear distinguishing factors the poetry genre is eventually lost altogether" in her monograph *Six Poetry Formats and Transforming Image* (University of the Philippines Press, 2007).

I tried to comfort myself that Madam M is a product of her own time—an old-school Marxist (the kind that has never heard of 'intersectionality'), aesthetically archaic, politically progressive. But it never escaped me: Madam M was a creative writing professor, a revolutionary essayist and poet (*revolutionary,* in her own time, at least) who wrote in English and in at least two other Philippine languages, and whose release from imprisonment during the Marcosian regime was celebrated by writers like Audre Lorde, Nadine Gordimer, Noam Chomsky, and others from across the globe. But locally, she judged book awards and literary prizes, paneled in writers workshops, mentored creative writing students in the undergraduate and graduate levels, among other things. And yet, her pronouncements on craft are very much outdated—as well as her judgements. But in my country, she is not the only older writer who keeps proclaiming things which are no longer applicable, as if they were in the first place.

But would it be safe to say that some people have been living in a bunker, not reading the latest writings—both theories and praxis—on craft?

. . .

Because you could not tell what was fiction and what was autobiography, what was poetry and what was prose.

from Kazim Ali's *Bright Felon* (2009), a prose poem, detective story, and place essay

. . .

Although the prose poem originated from French *poème en prose* as advocated by the Symbolists (Baudelaire, Mallarmé, Verlaine, Rimbaud, Valery) in late 1800s France where the Alexandrine was the dominant form, it could be traced to other literary traditions outside the Francophone terrain under various nomenclatures: the Graeco-Roman *prosimetrum*, the Turko-Persian *maqāmah*, the German *Prosagedicht*, the Chinese *sanwenshi*, the Japanese *sanbunshi*[2], the Arabic *qaṣidat al-nathr*, among others. American poet James Tate called it "a deceptively simple packaging: the paragraph." Or, as Chinese American poet Chen Chen would tweet, "i love prose poems. they're just like, i'm a paragraph. but different!!!!!" In an *Arab Lit* interview, essayist and translator Huda J. Fakhreddine would say, "All our translations [from Arabic to English] are prose poems."

From the French Symbolists to the British Decadent movement (Ernest Dowson, William Sharp, Oscar Wilde) to the 20th century Nahda modernist poets who defied against the measure of Arabic poetry—the meter—the prose poem, in at least three literary traditions, has radical histories. As for the American literary

6

landscape, it is theorized that "the prose poem [aligns] with 'working-class discourse' undermining the lyric structures of the upper bourgeoisie ... stress[ing] the inclusiveness of the genre."[3] In a *Newcastle Writers Festival* podcast, poet and co-editor of *Anthology of Australian Prose Poetry* (2020) Cassandra Atherton thinks of the genre as a "political little box."

But would it be safe to conclude such is the case with the others?

...

How, then, to define the prose poem? After reading so many, I can only offer the simplest common denominator: a prose poem is a poem without line breaks. Beyond that, both its manner and its matter resist generalization ... Surveying the 175 years of poetry represented here, what emerges for me is the prose poem's wayward relationship to its own form – and it is this, I believe, that makes it the defining poetic invention of modernity.

from Jeremy Noel-Tod's introduction to *The Penguin Book of the Prose Poem* (2018)

...

My nine-year-old nephew once asked me while I was writing.

"What's this?" he pointed to the screen.
"It's a poem. I'm writing one." His forehead creased.
"It looks weird," his eyes fixed on the right side of the 'paragraph,'
"No rhyme."

End of scene.

...

In an interview with ABS-CBN News, Conchitina "Chingbee" Cruz, author of *Dark Hours* (University of the Philippines Press, 2005) confessed, "Strangely enough, this book won a [Philippine]

National Book Award when it came out. [But] on more than one occasion I have been told by a member of that board, 'Pinag-awayan namin iyan kasi prose poetry iyan.' Sabi ng iba, 'Tula ba iyan?'"

"I think that kind of question is exciting to me because it urges you to rethink what a poem means, which I think keeps poetry alive," Cruz added.

> *Sabi ng iba, 'Tula ba iyan?'*
> *The others asked, 'Is that a poem?'*
> *Ingon ang uban, 'Balak gyod na?'*

...

But would it be safe to say that the prose poem is necessarily defiant?

Nick Admussen, in *Recite and Refuse: Contemporary Chinese Prose Poetry* (2016), pointed otherwise. Subversion, for Admussen, is "not necessarily [true] as in the case of non-English, non-French prose poetry." In mid-1900 mainland China, prose poems became tools for the "reaffirmation of Communist ... truths bursting forth ... an imaginative recapitulation and gesture of support for a nation's dominant political ideology." The same is the case of Russian prose poetry which originated from short parables, an evidence of the Minimalist movement's preference for the anti-story.

But would it be safe to say that the prose poem, along with other permutations of literary works such as the anti-narrative novels, epistolary poetry, fictocriticism, poems-in-memoirs (or memoirs-in-poems), and the lyric essay, rose to fame once again because of the contemporary times' preference for works that defy generic categorizations along with the surge of digital platforms, when literary traditions in Greece, the Caribbean, Africa, east Asia, and Syria, to name a few, have long had nomenclatures for poems without line breaks?

In *A Poetry Handbook* (1994), Mary Oliver claims, "The prose poem is too recent a form to have developed a tradition." A lot to unpack from this pronouncement—one of which is erasure. Anything that does not conform within the Anglophone and Western subjectivities of genre should not be labeled as hybrid, or new, or avant-garde.

The West is not the world.

...

On one of our thought-challenging exercises for Dialectical Behavioural Therapy, I would confess that I never considered myself a poet despite the fact that majority of my published works are poetry—not nonfiction, or works of translation, or author interviews, or reflections on the craft. I felt that 'poet' as a term is applicable to a certain kind of lifestyle. "Maybe that identity crisis is going to change after you publish a poetry collection, *no*?" my therapist replied. That was mid-2020 when everything happened via Zoom and I was in the midst of a string of month-long manic and depressive episodes.

When my collection came out in August 2021 still in the middle of "one of the world's longest covid-19 lockdowns" according to *TIME* magazine, the self-doubt as a poet was even greater.

...

The godfather of creative nonfiction Lee Gutkind considers prose poems, more or less, under the creative nonfiction umbrella: "in fact, the border between sudden [sometimes *brief* or *flash*] nonfiction and the prose poem remains murky and under dispute" (*Keep It Real*, 2008) and "creative nonfiction does not strictly adhere to one narrative form; there's the lyric essay, the segmented essay, and the prose poem, all of which can be nonfiction" (*You Can't Make This Stuff Up*, 2012).

Creative Nonfiction magazine, the journal-turned-magazine he founded, accepts prose poems as submissions and offers online classes on the prose poem along with the lyric essay.

The 2017 issue of *The Essay Review*, the journal of the University of Iowa's Nonfiction Writing Program, which is dedicated to "the essay's limitations and possibilities," published a sequence poem in mostly lineated verse.

. . .

> While fully aware of the functions of and corresponding pleasures derived from the line, I am interested in the prose poem, that is, poetry that does away with verse ... Other readers have gone so far as to reject the possibility of reconciling poetry and prose ... A milder form of skepticism is exhibited in my own poetry workshop classes, where the identity as a poem of a draft written in verse, no matter how badly written, is rarely (or never) viewed with suspicion, yet the "poem-ness" of a draft written in prose, no matter how promising and engaging, is bound to be—however gently—questioned."

from Conchitina Cruz's autocritical essay "'Without Contraries is no progression:' Reading the Prose Poem" published in the *Journal of English and Comparative Literature* 9: 1 (2006).

. . .

I never consciously thought of my own poetics in writing the pieces for my debut poetry collection. It was only after I read books on autotheory that I was able to do so. After all, I never intended it to be a collection. I guess organic is always the best route. But I do the usual hard work: I read, write, revise, and repeat it. I let friends read and comment on it. I send to publications where I think they fit when I'm confident enough, or even when I'm not. But if there is one, I must say my formula is lyricism using accessible language, and a metaphor or some other device that makes the piece transcend from an ordinary paragraph(s), lifting it to the level of literature if there is such a higher plane. Just like the lyric essay, "tightly packed language ... quick scenes, and ... concise imagery," as advised by Dinty W. Moore. Or, as Rigoberto González wrote, "[the] vehicle is sensory imagery, and [the] tenor is emotional experience." No need for narrative arc, no need for a story-driven plot. In publications, so much depends on editorial taste and aesthetic preference which are highly subjective.

But what worked for me may not work for another writer.

...

On Google, when one researches on the prose poetry tradition in the Philippines, there isn't much one can find. Search results range from the American Commonwealth anthology series *Philippine Prose and Poetry*, a published suite of prose poems by a few writers, occasional blog entries of aspiring ones, studies on the literary canon, a feature article by an older writer *simping*—to borrow from TikTok English—a younger one which is borderline creepy.

In the guidelines of some publications and writing fellowships, poetry submissions are measured in number of lines, not in pages. And that's telling, a subtle 'You're not welcome here!' But I know a lot about exclusion. I lived through it. Maggie Nelson, in a 2013 *Gulf Coast* roundtable discussion with essayists Eula Biss and Sarah Manguso on genre, lamented "I've grown so tired of writers ... pillorying that which they don't naturally tend towards."

A few scholars proclaim that Saint Augustine of Hippo's *Confessions*, the West's first important autobiography, takes the shape of prose poems addressed to God. I'm unsure if these are the same scholars who were unsettled with the subtitle of Edgar Allan Poe's book-length *Eureka: A Prose Poem*. I honestly do not know what to make of these.

British human geographer and poet Tim Creswell, despite acknowledging that "the boundaries between criticism, prose, and poetry have been blurred," still called Claudia Rankine's *Citizen: An American Lyric* "segmented prose paragraphs," while Maggie Nelson's body of work are "discrete, sometimes numbered text blocks [and] critical-creative engagements" in *Maxwell Street: Thinking and Writing Place* (2019).

My favorite definition of the prose poem is from Russell Edson: "A poetry freed from the definition of poetry, and a prose free of the necessities of fiction; a personal form disciplined not by other literature but by unhappiness; thus a way to be happy."

But I am not a happy person. *See Edson's essay "Portrait of the Writer as a Fat Man: Some Subjective Ideas or Notions on the Care and Feeding of Prose Poems." See my results in the Davidson Trauma Scale.*

...

Consider this tale of two letters—first, an acceptance from a Richmond, Virginia-based press' anthology of place poems:

> "Prose like yours is sometimes difficult to determine if it is also poetry, but you did a nice job of bringing to your poem the rhythm and flow of poetry within your prose paragraphs. The language in your poem is exquisite, the emotion and subject matter very intense."

Without giving author compensation, said press only promised me "publication credit, an opportunity to reach a broad audience, and my thanks." Still, it was my fault I submitted. But would I be at absolute fault when there are very few print anthologies which are dedicated to place writing, let alone place poems?

And this rejection from an international poetry journal based in the Devon, England:

> "I am not a fan of what I consider an oxymoron: prose cannot be poetry, only poetic—though often poetry can sound very dull and like a great deal of prose. Sorry."

At least, she apologized.

…

What demarcates the prosaic poetry from the poetic prose? From the prose poem? Or are a lot of works, as Tiempo suggested, merely "prose preening as poetry"? Maybe Madam M was half-right: poems are for emotions, essays are for ideas.

But consider this:

> *"Verse," a mode, is not equivalent to "poetry," a genre. To ask the question "What is the difference between prose and poetry?" is to compare anchors with bullets.[4]*

and

> *....the mutability of prose poetry as an appellation and a genre ... as a way of arguing that what coheres around genres is not an ideology, a lineage of influence, or even a set of formal restrictions, but a web of hermeneutic methods, a habit of grouping similar works that allows readers to understand the texts they read.[5]*

…

> *Sabi ng iba, 'Tula ba iyan?'*
> *The others asked, 'Is that a poem?'*
> *Ingon ang uban, 'Balak gyod na?'*

END NOTES:

The title is taken from Charles Simic's "Essay on the Prose Poem" delivered in 2010 at The Poetry Festival in Rotterdam: "For me, [prose poetry] is a kind of writing determined to prove that there is poetry beyond verse and its rules." Simic wrote *The World Doesn't End* (1989), the first collection of prose poems which won a Pulitzer Prize.

[1] In the early 1960s, Edith L. Tiempo, together with her husband, the novelist and critic Edilberto K. Tiempo, founded the Silliman University National Writers Workshop, a "direct reproduction of [Iowa Writers Workshop] in the Philippines … with Rockefeller [Foundation] money … one of the most important conduits through which New Criticism circulated throughout the Philippines," according to Paul Nadal in "Cold War Remittance Economy: US Creative Writing and the Importation of New Criticism into the Philippines" (published in the Fall 2021 issue of *American Quarterly*).

[2] The haibun, in the words of German scholar of Japanophone literature Agnes Fink-von Hoff's 2006 book *Petitessen, Pretiosen: die Prosaminiatur in Japan um 1910*, is more or less, poetic prose, not prose poem; literally "prose to accompany a haiku," or in some cases, haiku-like prose. See also *The Modern Japanese Prose Poem: An Anthology of Six Poets* (1980, Princeton University Press), featuring Miyoshi Tatsuji, Anzai Fuyue, Tamura Ryuichi, Yoshioka Minoru, Tanikawa Shuntaro, and Inoue Yasushi, translated and with an introduction by Dennis Keene.

[3] from David Lehman's *Great American Prose Poems: From Poe to the Present* (Scribner, 2003).

[4] from Lewis Turco's *The Book of Forms: A Handbook of Poetics, 3rd edition* (University Press of New England, 2000).

[5] from Nick Admussen's "The Chinese Prose Poem: Generic Metaphor and the Multiple Origins of sanwenshi," in *The Edinburgh Companion to the Prose Poem*, eds. Mary Ann Caws and Michel Delville (Edinburgh University Press, 2021); also see Steven Monte's *Invisible Fences: Prose Poetry as a Genre in French and American Literature* (University of Nebraska Press, 2000), Nick Admussen's *Recite and Refuse: Contemporary Chinese Prose Poetry* (University of Hawaii Press, 2016), Jane Monson's *British Prose Poetry: The Poems Without Lines* (Palgrave Macmillan, 2018), Huda J. Fakhreddine's *The Arabic Prose Poem: Poetic Theory and Practice* (Edinburgh University Press, 2021), and Cassandra Atherton and Paul Hetherington's *Anthology of Australian Prose Poetry* (Melbourne University Press, 2020).

You live in me. Malignant.

from "Hesitate to Call", Louise Glück

You might as well know nothing is free of you:
When I herd these tribes and fashion cities
With my words, you are what's missing.

from *Proxy Eros,* Mookie Katigbak-Lacuesta

Even now, I trespass in your name.

from *Spirit Lake*, Carl Phillips

Is it possible for this not to be a story of disappearance?

from *Dark Hours*, Conchitina Cruz

M IN THREE ACTS: PROLOGUE

i.   D'MORVIE SUITES
           Yacapin-Capistrano Streets

No, we've never been here together in our *dry* seasons. In 2017, an ex made me a makeshift glory hole and rehearsed it here. God knows how many times you checked in this landscape of the stale. We could have helped each other out.

Searing songs of cadence to the long bygone dusk, our *footsteps will fall.*[1] I hear your pulse, the hum in your sleeping throat, behind the wooden doors. The *dripdripdrip* of water from the AC, a car honks by the parking lot.

Let it be said that I want you to open my mouth and make it your quarry of rituals. Let it be asked, *who deserves rescue and who deserves to suffer?*[2]

I once signed up on Grindr with the hopes of chatting with you outside Facebook Messenger or SMS. I would nonchalantly say, "Omigod, you're here! Small world." And I would propose that while we are here, why not... but that's a story that never happened. The thing is, I can still imagine you standing serenely but with eyes of a kid in his first time at the mall, leaning on the receptionist's desk, asking where a particular room is.

I could only wish it was me with you, not another fellow orphan of touch. I, too, seek the origin of warmth.

Although, you won't ask that. You know this place so well, each crack on the floor, each stink of the sink, each stain in the walls. You reside in this transience, where restarts happen every 12 hours. This is your tradition.

v

         KATHRYN BAKESHOP
                Rizal-Abejuela Streets

You end the day at the usual spot, the same exact one, by the sidewalk fronting a bakery that sells thrifted chiffon cakes which you once considered buying for Mother's Day, and coconut bread. My mind imagines you being allergic to the latter but what do I know? Tonight, like any other night, a long ride to your side of the city. But thankfully, the jeepney drivers of the Bugo route drive like maniacs. That's their assigned character trope.

"Is working for a government agency worth it?" I would ask you. You pretend to fish something in your sling bag overstuffed with office paper works. I could not remember your answer—you may have mumbled *bureaucracy* and *salary grade* and *job order*—if you did answer at all. *This is why we are so lonely.*[1]

If there's a drizzle, you'd open the thrifted umbrella you bought from a boutique. This night looks copied from some Scandinavian noir. In a workshop, we learn, a year apart, that the lyricism of the word becomes a remedy for the dullness of life. Or so the septuagenarian writers who learned from American New Critics would say.

Sometimes, the commute traversing the length of Velez Street. Sometimes, *desire in a poem sounds like whining.*[2] Sometimes, the passersby are faceless. ~~*All desire is yearning*~~[3] and I still half-resent you for that.

I must confess: where the faded pedestrian lane lead to the concrete benches, where the homeless sleep, I would pretend and lie and make stories and delude you. A redemptive narrative arc doesn't apply to me. But know there is some truth to that: I mask people as places. So when I say *city*, I mean *you*, always you. Aren't we living in some Richard Siken poem—one of those from *Crush*?

Once gone from your vision, the city lights will fade, like in a stage play, as it always does when you're not looking. The passersby are, after all, faceless flat characters in a hubris drama where you are the de facto protagonist. I would retreat back to the grim fable where I come from. All of this that you see, hanging on a knife-edge standstill, will be curtained. Then, a whole void.

[1] From Vivek Shraya's *She of the Mountains.*
[2] From Richard Siken's essay "Why".
[3] *Do not, however, make the mistake of thinking that all desire is yearning.* From Maggie Nelson's *Bluets.*

iii.   TERRAZZO BAR
Tiano Brothers-San Agustin Streets

The dead end of the road in sight, we question
something else—

The uprising of our ghost-breaths in the mist,
aftermath of the downpour, that *rises above things
and names*[1]*:* ginger vodka, aluminum tong soaked in
cold water, your phone that keeps on vibrating, a
half-bottle of tequila, kropek.

Spared from the gesture of being a sketch of flawed
departures, *this is the difficulty of the nonbeliever:
waking, every morning, without a god.*[2] Today, your
horoscope says you are missed.

But know I have the affinity to screw things up, to
create pitfalls, to succumb to my demons.

Do not mistake me for a burning light when I am
just a pitless ruin.

---

[1] From Mahmoud Darwish's "To Describe an Almond Blossom".
[2] *I call this the difficulty of the non-believer, / Or, put another way, waking, every
morning, without a god.* From Donika Kelly's "Sanctuary".

PORTRAIT OF M AS DAYLIGHT

after Agnes Martin's 'Untitled No 1' (1981)

Now I know, daylight, like a yearning for skin, or a song, is free, like a sin offering. Outside this bestiary, this chimeric skyscape, is a faint memory from the homeland—dictate of chainsaw as it cuts through coconut trunk or vertical rain etched against a nation of white assuming the shape of ink. So I try to name you in the only ways that I know, seeking refuge on silence, the chasm. Free from the destiny to twirl, or to bob like a wave, or the way breeze gathers in your eyelashes, that marries your breath. Faint highlighter pen on grocery list, clipped and folded inside a wallet, forgotten from the years, spared from the repetition of hues. Dear calligraphy of light, devoid of many colors, but nonetheless alive, you are now but a lingering thief of the muted after. Time to speak of this quietude.

AN ANIME, A WAR, AND A DANCE: GAY BOYHOOD IN THREE SANBUNSHI

i. A playmate named D with gapped front teeth sits beside you, sweaty brows above his perpetually teary eyes, his slippers yanked in his elbows, some caked dust in his knee. You imagine smelling D's nape. This begins your age-old patterns: liking soft boys with tooth gaps and imagining smelling their dark napes. It is 4 in the afternoon, in the late 90s, or early 2000s. All the kids in pre-cable television, pre-Internet homes are glued to some afternoon anime. Recca, the last of the Hokage ninjas, summons his eight flame dragons: Resshin, Rui, Koku[1], Nadare, Homura, Saiha, Setsuna, Madoka. All of you—even your teenager-cousins—recite in chorus like a litany. Another neighbor who sits on the floor claims he is Recca and that starts a brawl. Unlike the others, you always relate to the villain-brother, Kurei, no, you always relate to the villain. But in your head, you and D are making out, wanting to recreate that *Fushigi Yuugi* poster where Tamahome stands behind Miaka, both naked and only clothed by leaves. D is Recca, or Tamahome. Or you are. You are so close to him that you see how his eyelashes flutter, how his eyes wonder at the screen before him. You feel the pulse in his neck, the breathing in this throat, warmer and warmer.

ii. What the JDoramas or any J-Pop song don't tell you is already in textbooks.

You sit with the first J, a gangly, brown-skinned guy, in high school Philippine history class. You quiz each other, after lunch, on comfort women, the imperial army's sex slaves in the Second World War, abducted from their husbands, their parents, their children, and the 'comfort stations' located in some parts of the country including the city where you live.

You watched the first hentai you've seen in his laptop, the first live-action porn with, disappointingly, the actor's blurred penis.

Your greatest heartbreak in high school wasn't the breakup with the student council vice president whom you, the school publication editor-in-chief, dated for mutual convenience. Your greatest heartbreak in high school was seeing typically shy J slow dancing with someone else at prom. *You weren't aggressive enough.*

The second J with the same lanky build and skin color would show up in a college Asian literature class where you read Lady Sarashina, Noh theater, the undertones of transgenderism in *Ranma ½*, Hiromi Itō, the difference between the haibun and the sanbunshi.

The day you learned that Japanese soldier-ghosts have owned a rightful place in local horror cinema and ghostlore, their displaced hands grabbing whatever it can hold on to in some small-town rivers, their dismembered heads wandering in and out in some old hospital hallway, was also the same day you asked J out. He tells you he's straight. And that it meant a different thing to you from the very start.

He says you guys could stay friends. But he now sits at the front row, away from you. *You were too aggressive.*

iii. In a college party themed throwback 90s, the DJ plays Pizzicato Five and Globe. B, the nerdy boy with curls in glasses who has never said a word to you, suddenly grabs you for a dance. Tipsy, you could no longer gather the karaoke lyrics you used to memorize by heart: *Hora revue ga hajimaru / hora okurenaide ne / hora revue ga hajimaru / hora wasurenaide ne.* Tipsy, you remember your tragic high school prom: *Feel like dance itsu no koro ka / akirame kaketa yume mawari mawaru / chansu ga ajike nai hodo toorisugiteku yo.* You both slipped into an awkward slow dance but the lights from the disco ball frame B's handsome face and his Recca otaku getup for the night. You think of acting out with a boy you never *saw* before. You rest your chin in his shoulders, your cheek against his neck. *Too aggressive.* But you also think of the illusions of potential, the risks of falling into same old patterns. You excuse yourself for a bathroom break. *Not aggressive enough.* Isn't this the hilarity of well-wrought living? No one knows exactly when is the time for restraint, to let things simmer on their own, and when to confront things as you face them, to dance as if it is the last. You leave B in the dance floor. You never return.

QUESTIONS

A neighbor's cemented fence cuts through a chunk of the wingspan one-way road. At the corner, a makeshift grill of banana coated with margarine beside one of the neighborhood's sundry stores, a cockpit, a crowd of rickshaw drivers, some barefoot children holding their slippers, street dogs with eczema. Tonight, this street will dim yellow, casting jaundice on concrete. *Did you once bring a lover here and introduce them as your friend?*[1] This is the same road you tread on as your Grindr app was active, as you checked *who's nearby*. And as you pick your way, the bulb light from someone else's front porch and streetlight above another's railing. Have you taken your dose of antihypertensives after breakfast? Locate the rural within the urbansphere, urged the ecocritics. Google Weather says 39 degrees Celsius will peak at noon just in time for your lunch break. But it always rains before nightfall. The weather bureau declares La Niña. Last night, in the island where I live, a lightning bellowed over a southern mountain. It afforded the landscape of a blink of daylight. Are you still afraid of thunder? The midday sun here, too, is harsh. They warned us of heat stroke. Hypertension runs in my family, too. And so does schizophrenia. I tell my shrink about you. He nods and jots down a string of words in his notepad. Is this a new template for some therapy meme? A sling bag on your hunched right shoulder, uncertain. Strolling along a busy street—either RN Abejuela Street or Corrales

Avenue—but actually dreaming of sitting by a lakeside house like in a movie or a long overdue mountaineering trip. The mayor boasts of the statistics like some messiah. He mentions vaccination rate and number of deaths repeatedly, proud like a coach as if he alone has made this possible. Is it now safe for hookups? I think I saw you once in a photo on alter Twitter, behind someone else, him covering his face with his phone, and you covering yours with your right hand, your left anchored at the back of his hips. Both of you fronting a mirror. I had a hard-on. In another city, I pass by a mosque on the left, a warehouse of canned meat on the right. Farther, a factory of junk food, a subdivision of unfinished housing units. *I thought I saw you at the bus stop, I didn't though.*[2] Half-naked boys gather at one of the road's six lanes. This was on the day Adele released a song after six long years. In another lifetime, I turn out to be a revenant. *Much can never be redeemed.*[3] My malaise of a chest returns as a gap of mistakes.

[1] *You meet some woman on the internet and take her home.* From Taylor Swift's "the 1".
[2] Also from Taylor Swift's "the 1".
[3] From Mary Oliver's "Don't Hesitate".

LETTERS TO M: FIVE SCENES

2019

I dreamt of you five times since the last time we saw each other in July, also the last time I shaved my pubes. In a dormitory where we share the same double-deck bed. In a classroom where we were seatmates and I refuse to talk to you. In a hospital where I brought you fruits and chicken stew, and we held hands in front of your mother. In my apartment where you caught me in the shower. In a conference room where you asked me where I will go for lunch.

In real life, you tell me about a hookup—*I thought you don't fuck femmes*. He's not even attractive, was my thought. In real life, you tell me about a date—*I thought you aren't into bitches*. The poem he wrote you after your supposed one-night stand isn't even a poem, was my thought.

Somewhere between waking and sleep, I check the compatibility of our Greek zodiac signs, our MBTI personality types. I hit replay on your second most played song on Spotify.

2018

> A *bálak*, a poem written in our native tongue,
> starts with the pastoral imagery,
> age-old rhyming schemes, line breaks,
> alluding to the shapes of the female body,
> all in usual misogyny, the male gaze.
> You tell me that the poet whom you met once
> was creepy. I reply, *And so was the editor.*
> After reading Glück's "Hesitate to Call,"
> I tell a friend about you: *You live in me. Malignant.*

2020

In a roadside motel along Barra, I meet up with Anthony and Von,
their alter names. Anthony's eyes remind me of yours when they
gain insight. Von's smell is from the same brand of your body wash
I pretend to not like. Sometimes we invite someone named Chris,
always fresh from his shift. He has the same profession as you. We
fuck every time I am in town.

2017

Has it been said that the *búsaw*,
bloodthirsty demon-spirit, is notorious
for hiding souls of the ill inside the sun?
And so the B'laan try to appease it
in the ways that they know:
Magkalikag sang Ilawan,
magkasang sang Tiwayan,
the heavens have been disturbed,
the skies are confused, chants the priestess
in her gingham cotton blouse
and tubular skirt, the veins of her neck
showing against her pale skin,
against the balefire. I want to say celestial,
heavenly, I want to say honor, as I imagine
the búsaw snatching me
in the middle of the night,
sucking my blood, emptying my will,
weakening my all. Isn't death a destination?
I wait beyond this night, I blur from sight
as I recite the búsaw's name
like a forbidden prayer, like a secret code,
fronting the altar of an offering,
a pig adorned with sallapaw tree leaves
and betel nut flowers.
Dear advocate of plague,
eat all of me. In a cove along Lake Sebu,
as I face the false start of sunrise,
a refusal of drought, I no longer think of the búsaw.
I think about your elbow against mine
in an armrest of a movie house.

2021

In the port of Dapa, a midday drizzle, I think about us strolling along the stretch of Pabayo Street at nightfall. I pretend to write about the police checkpoints and long lines of vehicles and commuters in the eastern border of our city when all I intended was to write about you, imagining you as you wait for a jeepney ride home in one of the street alleys near a bakery, a convenience store, and what used to be a gay bar.

In a porn clip, three white girls give a blow job to a lean Taiwanese guy. He has the same body build as you. Does he have the same nipple color as you have? Same dishevel in the hair of your pits? My guess is yes. I zoom his upper body in. I have never seen you half-naked. I jerk off to that video once a week.

MIDWEEK RAIN

It is midweek, the sun is supposed to cast its afterglow at the ruins called city, only this time, it is rain water. *The same rain claims your morning run.*[1] I imagine you, again, in a sweater you never wore or even bought. You are inside the office you work for when you looked momentarily at the window as the first of the drizzle swarms from a clear afternoon sky dashing on the nearby vacant lot. The inner child in you presses his cheeks against the glass in wonderment, recognition: *the past, rainy evenings like this in your birth month, me.* A grandmother you miss once told you a secret: when it rains while the sun is up, a feast in the heavens. In my grandmother's garden, I hunted the dragonflies and damselflies to extinction. Further, Julio Pacana Street, in a rush, like a river. Two of them—the rivers of Iponan and Cugman—are in overflow, said the local radio. But you've no words for things as they take shape: the waters that pass each downtown bridge before the bay, the way headlights illuminate raindrops for half a second, and later today, the wholeness of the blue hour. I don't know which months end in the 31st. So when the weather bureau said the northeast monsoon season has begun in a news you didn't bother to read or hear, you only brought a sweater. *These are parts of your body that I will never know.*[2] Aren't we alone in the places we inhabit—office cubicles, bodies, motel rooms? I could give you heat of open fire. For now, the dark of your nape, your frame of a body endures the cold.

[1] *A hunger claims your morning run.* From Jody Chan's "semantic satiation".
[2] *There are parts of our bodies we will never know.* From Sarah Westcott's "Bud".

from 'THE BOOK OF ETIQUETTE FOR FUCK BUDDIES'

i. I know you
by the many names
you use for camouflage:
fbuds, blow bud, Netflix and chill,
bennifriends, "maintenance," white boy toy, *afam.*

ii. It would be as if we had labels: / how we would lay atop each
other's body / —flesh of oyster hinged on its shell— / for hours,
how we would converse / over cigarettes about the abstract depth /
after it. We both prefer Marlboro Ice Blast, / "the brand for
construction workers and security guards," / said some pretentious
poet-wannabe.

iii. Always, the bland air freshener of motel rooms, stained thin
blankets on uncomfortable beds, thrifted sachets of shampoo and
toothpaste, a strand or two of your naturally blonde hair on the
pillows, thin bars of that soap brand promising 100% skin germ
protection as if it can be cleansed from us at all.

iv. Always, I leave first. But this time, you offered a ride home.
"Are you my Uber driver now?" Instead, along the lonely
highway between General Luna and Del Carmen, in between
quarantine checkpoints, you decided to recite a line that has
haunted you knowing I was some exiled poet with a dark past. (I
expected Goethe or Rilke.) Richard Siken, you lectured in your
guttural English, once wrote, "You are feeling things he's no
longer in touch with." I knew the poem by heart but I only wanted
a *versa,* not a verse.

v. And finally, / the design of digital nonchalance: / unseen chats, unreturned calls, ghostings of the living. This / is how you hunt me. *But / I cannot give what I do not have,* was all / I said. The rule we both created / in our compact of bodily fluids: Always, / there shall be no care, only craving. / This is how you haunt me: wet dreams / of shared shower baths, your musk still / on my shirt.

vi. To my little feast,
I cannot invite you in. Hunt,
haunt. I cannot let you
partake in this
wreckage.

IN A DREAM

a flicker of fireflies gather around your head, their jointed legs tiptoeing in the tips of your curly hair, *lingering like smoke.*[1] To the Mamanwa, the dream means you staying in me. Your body wash, a smell I no longer remember. How can I miss something I have forgotten? *I was never skilled at forgetting.*[2] Absence makes the heart grow fonder, the cliché goes, but abandonment heightens anger. I am afraid that this rage in me is what will stay long after yearning left. I hear the humming in your chest, the hammering in your throat as you sleep. Your sweaty hands, a remnant of rain's whisper, in the small of my back. You see, in here, nothing makes sense. They don't have to. *I say a thing out loud and it becomes less potent.*[3] But I am sober, the kind of sobriety only orgasm affords. Do you still jog at the oval after office hours wearing worn black shoes and clumsy shorts? I asked, like a memorized dialogue from a play. The prompt: How to know that a cramped room has long been abandoned? A cobweb without a spider, dry leaves in the window pane, heaps of dust. I say, appeal to the five senses: The dusk clouds are Aegean ships, sailing through a cerulean sea. Rain drop on tin roof, repeated and repeated like a chorus of things, or a drone claiming a corner in my side of the city. The ecocritics categorize *wilderness* from *scenic sublime* from *countryside* from *domestic picturesque.* Thus, an abandoned airport is a grassland of devil weeds interrupted by concrete. A banana leaf bows down to earth, a finch sits on its midrib, like paperweight putting it in place. A fruit bat swings like a pendulum in the roof's gutter as annoying as a hair strand stuck in the tip of the tongue. The smoke from burned books by poets you used to hang out with turns out to be pungent, stings the eyes. Everything else you hear, earthborn, *balaan, balaan, balaan, sa tanan ikaw giludhan, dinuko tanang galamhan hangtud kadagatan,*[4] old Catholic tune, the kind that's still sung in little chapels of little hinterland villages. In this dream, there are two of us: you, the center of the gaze, and me, the mere voyeur. A dating app says I'm 32 kilometers away from you. *I can love the distance between us. I can.*[5] I leave. Take my place.

[1]*Lingering like smoke*. From Golnoosh Nour's "Lost Cult".
[2]*you were never skilled at waiting*. From Jody Chan's "semantic satiation".
[3]*Because once you say a thing out loud it will often become less potent.* From Dinty W Moore's "Rivering".
[4]*holy, holy, holy, bowed down of all, all powers until the oceans kneel to you.* From a songbook of Iglesia Filipina Independiente, nationalist and independent Catholic Church of the Philippines which proclaimed schism from the Roman Catholic Church in 1902, translation mine.
[5]*I can love / the distance between us. / I can.* From Jody Chan's "stay at home order".

M OF THE SOUTHERN DOWNPOURS

"remembering / which I suppose is a form of missing"
Dorothea Grossman's "It is not so much that I miss you"

From the windshield, I see the damp stretch of this street, fallen leaves from narra trees of the Capitol Grounds here and there, forsaken papers of sort, a lost government form, crumpled receipts, a used lotto ticket, a candy wrapper crepe. When stepped on, they do not make a sound the way a twig cracks as fire consumes it. Of the before, I unclench my fist, take a deep breath, remain still.

I want to tell you all this in detail as if confessing a crime in death bed or to a journal entry. This is where you traverse going home. Everything in here, even the abandoned, are bluish, and no Google Map view could justify. Photographic memory, which is to say, *the ability to remember with the precision ... moment in full detail.*[1] Thus, I know the route so well, a pattern of what comes first, and then, what comes after: A hospital, a radio station, a century-old high school, a sports center, another hospital. Farther and farther, a traffic light that never works, a thrift shop of old things.

I mourn the passing of each vehicle—a jeepney that's half-full, a motorcycle with three passengers, the occasional ambulance, fancy cars. I notice the sound of the wheels wading through little floods from canal water that traces the crack of cement, then overflows. What are used to cover the head?, I asked, eyeing the sight like a journalist as if rain in itself could make some news beat. An umbrella, a raincoat, a jacket, a backpack, sometimes a face shield. I think of an accusation, like *poor urban planning* or *overpopulation* or *climate change*, and then shelve it for some tweet or an opinion think-piece to a local daily. It never rains like this on your birth month.

Somewhere in the loss, in the after, a hospital glass window caked with dust and mist mirror a nearby street light, a lone star shines in the eastern night skies after the southern downpour, your eye glasses reflect a headlight of a passing truck that looms over your shadow.

The imperative of yearning is to let it simmer and wind up in its haunt. After water, what will take its place? I weep, *eyes closed forever to find you.*[2]

This is how I pray now.

[1] From José van dijck's "Mediated Memories: Personal Cultural Memory as Object of Cultural Analysis" in *Continuum: Journal of Media & Cultural Studies* 18:2, 261-277 (2004).
[2] From Franz Wright's "The Poem".

CAR FUN OF HAND JOBS PAST

You put your finger in his mouth while he drives off of the mall's underground parking lot. He asked for it, part of the role play you agreed on: he's the Grab driver, you're the passenger, Fake Taxi-style, except that you're the one with motives, he's the innocent virgin about to be destroyed. For immersion, you watched a lot of clips from XVideos.com—it loads faster than PornHub.

From the way his lips curved, elastic wet muscle, you know he likes sucking something. (Mommy issues just like yours?) Your therapist warned you about dating guys with the same old issues—bullied as a kid, distant and disciplinarian father, low self-esteem—but you're drawn to routine, to sameness, and this is just a hook up anyway. In his fancy stereo, he plays Bebe Rexha and Cash Cash's "Take Me Home," your favorite sex song since then, your finger still in his mouth.

Chubby, facial beard in the jaw, semi-disheveled hair, nerdy, exactly your type. You weren't disappointed. Flabs over abs, someone who could lift you while he pumps hard, you tell a friend when asked about your type. You date everyone but the bigger, taller ones have a special place for you. Some Freudian need for physical security maybe, some deep-seated want to be protected from the cruel, cruel world, you hypothesized.

"Nice ride! Model?" you asked, trying to sound casual. Honda was the only name that registered. Talking about cars is a foreign language. But the funny thing was, he was wearing the same thing you wore, except for his glasses, your beanie, and the hoodie of his college you once fancied at the university bookstore: shirt, shorts, slippers, a watch. "We match!" he said as he pulls over near a factory by the highway.

He came in your palm as he nibbled your ear, his dick was a little curved on the side. He eyed you with an apologetic look:

for coming in your palm or for coming almost five minutes late after you did, you do not know. "No, it's fine," you assured him, wiping it with a tissue from the dashboard, "we won't see each other again anyway," you said coldly because you're a heartless bitch, to which he replied, "Yeah, sure," with a lilt in his voice. None of you will say a single word after that. The role play is over. You pretend to doomscroll on Twitter, a fascist who jokes about rape and admits killing people was going to be president. You have a troubled relationship with silence. You think this guy whose dick you wanted to suck might have voted for him.

He cups his hand in your lap, some sort of foreclosure, like Canova's "Theseus and the Minotaur," as if you were a cloth that needed ironing. But the funny thing was, in your language, the gayspeak for handjob is plantsa, literally ironing of clothes. You don't like touch after a hook up. You have a troubled relationship with touch. But you let him.

The engine whirs. In the dimness, you pass by a few drunkards preening themselves at a roadside karaoke bar, their shirts yanked in their shoulders. Then, it was silent again. Cugman, or the barangay named after the Spanish word for port or the last barangay of the city's border in the west? You do not know much of geography.

He did not offer a stick of cigarette like the others did. You do not know how to speak of this commonplace silence. The road trails behind you like the personal demons gnawing parts of you that you cannot hide. This city is burning.

PORTRAITS OF M IN A MILKING VIDEO

Cumming is easy but finding the right porn is hard, someone would tweet. But desire also insists itself in the form of wanting to lick another's almost hairless armpits as lean arms are raised as if in surrender, hands on top of his head as he sits on a white monobloc, anonymous in black cap and black mask. In the smooth of his oiled chest, you rest your tongue, down to the navel, he swallows his Adam's apple. *Milker* is what these anonymous hands, sometimes head, are named, and they *edge,* as if this was something sharp, painful. And in a way it is, as they jerk off after he has long came, long dripped in his inner thighs, a ritual of sort.

. . .

You encounter the word penis in 5th grade science class, its enormity chalked on the green board. Everyone giggles, even the teacher who drew it. In a copy of *Cosmo Philippines* owned by your aunt, it says *member* as if it follows. Or *manhood,* as if some metonymy for machismo. *I am mad about language.*[1]

. . .

What survives apart from the contingent dream of worshipping the feet? As empty as a motel room. *Al lado de la carretera, un pero hambriento hundía su cabeza en una bolsa de plástico negra.*[2] The road literally exhaling on you, the road just a spit away.

. . .

Someone uploads a photo of a hallway of a motel in a city 158 kilometers from where you are sitting, an invitation to *your makeshift raft to freedom.*[3] Scroll past a dictator's son that denies history. A gay couple trips on straight guys, a Grab driver, a pet shop employee, a flight attendant, a FoodPanda delivery guy, a random 18-year-old. My favorite is that of a balut vendor, moreno-skinned, the way his lean arms tense upon orgasm, walnut-colored nipples. *Raw and unprepared.* Or so the script says, like some spontaneous Big Brother show, just some old hungers of young men in the sovereign of shadows. Didn't they say the person who drinks the first dew that drops from banana heart on a full moon gains the strength of the world? And so I drink from yours, *a body I love.*[4]

[1] From Naomi Shihab Nye's "Israelis Let Bulldozers Grind To Halt".
[2] *By the side of the road, a famished dog sunk his head into a black plastic bag.* From Gaspar Orozco's "El libro de los Espejismos" (The Book of Mirages), translated from the Spanish by Ilana Luna.
[3] From Lu-Hai Liang's "We Are All Born In Water".
[4] *Only the poet sells his soul to separate it / from the body he loves.* From Tomaž Šalamun's "Folk Song," translated from the Slovenian by Charles Simic.

JAMES

after Carl Phillips' "Anywhere Like Peace"

I supposed it was only a back massage but when I turned over, you were already naked, lean but muscular, twink-*borta* in-betweener, my type—twunk delight!—except that you're fair-skinned like me and, no offense, seemingly unintelligent. You're hung, though, and too talkative, which are non-issues unless anal is involved but it will be. You tell me you're sorry for being late, *ser*. It was the heavy rain in Cogon and flood in Kauswagan, all over the city, you said, hushed like the thunderstorm outside. On TV, the mayor reminded us of the minimum public health standards in his daily Covid briefing but we've long removed our face masks, no face shields in sight. But know this: like this hometown which has grown alienating yet intruding, I was already wet and dirty. My "I'm only visiting for the holidays, "*migo*" to your "I'm still studying at the state university, *ser*." Your tongue (and teeth) in my left nipple and then, nape, the way I wanted you to—such mind-reader! Always, my grip in your ass. And when you tried to enter me—sexless for two years of Zoloft and Seroquel—you were already hard without porn-scrolling from a Grindr pic trade or *#AlterCDO* on Twitter. The extended child's pose, *Utthita Balasana*, meant something else now. But I must say, first time for me, average-looking as I am. Will I be fucked—and feel wanted—like this again, or am I stuck with you? But you see, I never confuse friendliness with flirting, or being horny with needing cash. There are still binaries, despite what the queer theorists say. In this, business is business. Take things at face value: I want you for your body—your palm on my back, your balls in my mouth—you want me for my money. Consumer rights intact, no labor law violated, win-win. Then, we both will walk away from this highway motel contented, you with my thousand peso bill, I with your cum. Only then can we brave this storm in a city which will never know.

CY

A guy is naked in my shower in a room assigned by the
receptionist who doesn't know I knew about the dead woman
found half-naked, hands tied in the same room, two years ago.

The guy doesn't have a name. I never asked. They always lie
about their age. But I call him Cy. Cy said he doesn't come fast.

Cy is now in my bed. So as I reside in his navel, the smell of baby
powder, I see your goatee in his chin, your jawline at the edge of
his.

You see, I desire strangers with parts of you: a porn actor with
your body build, an anonymous Grindr user with *your* name, a
passenger on the jeepney wearing *your* shoes, a mutual whose
tweets I read in *your* voice, someone on Tinder in *your* favorite
shirt.

At the back of this roadside motel, shadowed by a jackfruit tree
with its fruit wrapped in a sack, Cy and I smoke while three
generations of neighborhood mothers play mahjong behind a wall
topped with barbed wire or some shards of colored bottlesbroke
by their drunkard husbands.

The city says nothing beyond this limit, afraid some shards touch
the sky, cause a crash of an airplane we used to run after as kids.
*Los pájaros en los círculos abiertos del aire caliente. Los
humanos en los círculos abiertos del sueño. En el valle, las
sombras.*[1] Didn't they change the room numbers since the murder?
To confuse the living which room to avoid, to confuse the dead
which room to haunt.

And so he muffles my moans by covering my mouth, a silver in his ring finger jolting my tooth. I clench on his nape, some soft dark animal, easing the tremors of our own making. I always thought I was more of a breather, less a moaner. So I would not know the silence of the dead; I never visit them, they never visit me.

Sometimes I yearn for Cy, for men who are not you.

[1] *Birds in the open circles of hot air. / Humans in the open circles of dreams. / In the valley, the shadows.* From Gaspar Orozco's "El libro de los Espejismos" (The Book of Mirages), translated from the Spanish by Ilana Luna.

JESS

Already, LANY's "It Was Love" was playing on Magic 89.3 FM. This meant I'm now in the same region as you are. But no, we did not sing this song, never did. You hate this band, called them the Michael Faudet school of #momol anthem on bass. ***This is one love. There are many loves but only one war***. Instead, in someone's backseat, we tried M2M's "Don't Say You Love Me" together, two *desentonados* trying to find rhythm. ***You're in a car with a beautiful boy, and you're trying not to tell him that you love him.*** We were platonic, is the submerged backstory, unrequited love, too… which is to say creating unnecessary crisis. How to best move the plot forward, to set the opening in motion? ***Someone has to leave first. This is a very old story. There is no other version of this story***. In a workshop, I preached that landscapes resonate with emotional weathers. But back in my first summer in Siargao, I think of the rainy nights in Opol, the town that separates our cities. ***The seaside town. The electric fence***. Which scene to omit in the revising—the part where you lingered in my leg, your hand protectively in the small of my back or the part where you memorize some small details of my life I don't even think about? ***The fear: that nothing survives. The greater fear: that something does***. Old friend, your Trojan horses still live in me.

Lines in italics and bold are from Richard Siken's various poems.

DOMINIQUE

You leaned in to ask, almost like a whisper, eye to eye, *How's the blood pressure?* A vein of your lean moreno neck visible, emerging from your collared shirt marked "volunteer nurse," the face of the provincial governor at the back as if he made the vaccine himself. *Tacky*, was my comment on your uniform. Of course, I didn't say it aloud. I was pretending to scroll on social media, trying not to meet your glance, trying not to smell your masculine musk that penetrates through my face shield. *Opia*, according to The Dictionary of Obscure Sorrows, *is the ambiguous intensity of looking someone in the eye which can feel simultaneously invasive and vulnerable. Pumppumppump*, squeezing the bulb of the sphygmomanometer, pressing its cuff as it wraps my arm. Isn't this an emptied territory of touch when fingerprint meets skin pore? *Pumppumppump*, showing more veins in your wrists, more muscle in your skinny forearm. I probe their length. Isn't this a stronghold of infernal desire, the wanting to reach out and reciprocate? I no longer know. But dear nice guy in eye glasses, how we could do this all day, us playing pretend doctor and patient, except that we somehow are, in a vaccine facility. Such is a stuff of a foreplay though, or a scene lifted from clichéd gay porn. *A hundred twenty over eighty*, you said, writing it down in a list, to which I said, *Is that normal?* Of course, I played dumb. I subsist in nonchalance. And you, in the eyes like that of an actor from some Filipino romcom, said, *Yes!* Too enthusiastic, I must say. But anytime now, I must return to the story of the world outside this confined cold. *This has to be the last poem with you in it but other poems will be written, other men will be met, to take your place.*[1]

---

[1] *This is the last poem with the ocean in it / but other poems will be written to take its place.* From Bruce Snider's "This Is The Last Poem With The Ocean In It".

CATALOG OF CITY BOYS
WITH COMMON NAMES

Joey[1]
Camaman-an, Cagayan de Oro City

[1] This is, what's left, of you, in me: two lubed fingers, now three, then huge dick, all your inquiry into the body. Consider it as a vessel. Or a temple, Christ-sacred, like in the First Letter of Saint Paul the Apostle to the Corinthians. Chiseled chest, your obsession with men in uniform, now your lean pale arms spread out in the peninsula of the creased sheets. The drone of the air-conditioning, drowning your snores, insistent, echoing back to my side of the bed, like a dirge.

Ilja[2]

Berlin, Germany / Siargao Island, Surigao del Norte

---

[2] Worshipped your body, although your boobs tasted of deodorant. Your neck, a safe word. Your entirety, a permission. *Spankmemommylhavebeenabadbadboy.*

Mark[3], the Third

Gingoog City, Misamis Oriental / Malaybalay City, Bukidnon

---

[3] In my first week here in Malaybalay, renting an apartment of a sunny woman who fed us the best beef *lauya* for Sunday lunch. A year in, and I imagine you still, the sunbaked earth of May in your ankles after the dust bowl of a road kicking up dust, the lashes of your dreamy Piscean eyes reviling into memory, returning the stupor in the early morning quiet.

Osh[4]

Cairo, Egypt

---

[4] We always begin with place: pollen that evades your air purifier, petrichor that endures the touch of rain, all that triggers your allergic rhinitis. I tell you about the deities from *Moon Knight*: Khonshu, Ammit, Taweret. *Oscar Isaac is not even Egyptian or Arab,* I'd say. *It does rain in here, in the south, at least,* you'd tell me as I stare at the weather forecast on TV, the desensitizing sight of coastline expecting landfall. *At least two species of bananas grow in here, too,* you'd tell me as I cup shrimp paste to go with water-boiled sweet plantain for afternoon merienda. *Hmmmmm, never knew that before* but I actually do, I actually do. In the distance, a landscape of banana trees, waiting with dread for downpour.

Marc[5]

Rosario Crescent, Limketkai Center, Cagayan de Oro City

---

[5] Mr. Perfect-in-flesh, reads Marx and Didion, also psychic-astrologer, occasionally surfs. Virgo sun, Scorpio ascendant, Sagittarius moon. He taught me how to read tarot cards, how to interpret the universe speaking in codes. I taught him the little things I know about poetry. He thinks I'm *not like all the others, they're a long way down,* quoting his favorite Electric Guest song, singing that line out loud every time I ride shot gun in his fancy Ford. Was that a confession from someone conventionally attractive or is he just romanticizing a poet with a dark past? Named after the Roman god of war, his natal chart's ruling planet, he might just be the storm-safe of my homestretch. But we're not compatible: he loves to take so much space, I obsess over control. I can never again take in more Ms and Virgos and Ms who are Virgos. One of them has consumed my entirety. Dear reader, this is a story shelved for another lifetime, a parallel universe.

Ace[6]

Vamenta Boulevard, Carmen, Cagayan de Oro City

---

[6] …could have been The One with his lilting Surigaonon accent, faint patches of shadows under his eyes, and dimples that elongate when he smiles, his kind heart and sunny disposition (some premium standard I held but didn't know existed) but I never heard from him after samgyeopsal. *UrbanDictionary.com* tells me, reader, that I've been *soft ghosted.*

Jess[7]

National Highway, Barra, Opol, Misamis Oriental

---

[7] I could begin by saying he's the one who technically devirginized me, literally rummaged through me, being the first hookup after a sexless drought of two pandemic years. While he fatherly cradles me in his arms, Madonna sings and twirls in my head. And he's an ideal fuck buddy because I will never see him that way. *And why is that?*, a friend asks to which I said, *Well, he voted for a Marcos and a Duterte.* Ironic for someone named after a rebellious Jewish prophet, no? But nothing surprises me anymore, dear reader. Outside, the ghost of a hospital that was once a looming presence across the street, a tea shop turned parking lot. Even these bare, bland walls have witnessed: he doesn't let me lick his pits, he never kisses me on the lips during missionary.

V^8, the Second

Manolo Fortich, Bukidnon

---

[8] He taught you a lesson, a live hands-on: less teeth, more tongue. He could last for hours on top of you, he claims, and he actually could. All the while, an evangelist whose church endorsed two spawns of two dictators preaches about Leviticus chapter 18 on Sunday TV. When pressed, he tells you of an old, familiar plot: he is in love with a friend and you are a guilty distraction, or a tool for his little revenge, on the night before Valentine's. He asked you out for coffee after you shitted in his condom. You said sorry too many times. ~~This is an ongoing story.~~

Ivan[9]

Carmen, Cagayan de Oro

---

[9] His pits are without flaw. His upper body, a tribute to some pagan god of twunks.

He comes while you kiss, warm honey slurped from cold spoon without the little jolts in the teeth. Just coats and haunts in the throat. He kisses your forehead afterwards, the way the breeze of summerlong rain titillates what's between your eyebrows, tingling the lashes of your closed eyes. He is erotic nature poetry incarnate, ballad-became-body.

He says you're a good kisser as he leaves for the shower, as you put your briefs back on. And you believe him, you had to. Or else, you'd never know what else you're good at.

PJ[10]

Kauswagan & Pabayo, Divisoria, Cagayan de Oro City

---

[10] The walking and breathing evidence that some platonic friendships start out as a game called nipple play, although it wasn't exactly a hookup. It was more of him incessantly telling me of a guy from Twitter [*see footnote 5*], it was him kissing me torridly in between my licking of his huge, hairy nipples while he masturbates, it was him in some therapist couch while I listen. Some sort of mutual charity sex or mercy fuck for each other: he for his being broken, me for my loneliness. I'd find us both slouched at the fire exit, the panorama of an abandoned hotel that towers the city, the rainy suburb of green and gray surrounding us. On both our mouths, dear reader, lit cigarettes, their smoke lost in the mist of downpour.

Jeremy[11]
  Mintal, Davao City & Pala-o, Iligan City

---

[11] An apologist of storm you are, from a city rarely ravaged by one. *Perhaps you aren't seeing this the right way: rain is a blessing, a cleansing of what remained but should have gone*, you tell me as a storm gathers above a city both foreign to us. I said little, my replies, tone-deaf.

No poet has celebrated drought, you insist, left brow cocked, nostrils flared, *our thanks go skyward*, as if you are offering a slice of earth, the faint smell of craft beer from your mouth hanging in the air.

On my shoulder, your arm, swathing the stretch of Miguel Sheker avenue. In my ears, his name, your ex-boyfriend from back home.

Then this impending daybreak. Then I, fading into its Persian blue.
Then this downpour, a cold betrayal.

Mohammed Aji[12]

Sabala Manao, Marawi City

---

[12] *Can I borrow your plate?* were the first words he said to you. The pitch round of his eyes against the grey of his ruined city razed to the ground.

This is, of course, you both didn't want: the mosques in rubbles, his ancestral houses outlining absence, all of the terrain around everything he grew up with, a field of wreckage.

In a dare, you kissed the V-shaped skinful where his arm stops and his chest begins, leading to the pits, because he spelled Nietzsche right.

Samia Allah u liman hamidah, Rab'bana lakal hamd, you repeat in your head, repeat in your head after him for Fajr, refusing the rescue of daylight.

In the beginning was his name. And in the name, was his body.

Anthony[13]

Lapasan, Cagayan de Oro City

---

[13] You both danced to the beat of Dua Lipa on top of the bar stools in a now-abandoned Corrales Avenue discotheque. A bottle of gin in one hand, vape in the other. Letting loose, as if there is no tomorrow. And literally, there won't be. He's getting married. You're moving out of town.

YACAPIN STREET MOTEL

after "My Tears Ricochet" from Taylor Swift's folklore

Here, the ceiling bleeds water as if crying. The midday rain
dissipates the threat of bombs. The weather bureau avows on an
incoming weather disturbance. The TV only shows BBC World:
mosque burnings in London, the weather in Lahore, death of
refugees in Lagos.

Across the street, the owner of the diner does not let you pay for a
cup of rice, winks at you, and stutters as you order a bottle of
Pepsi. You settle in between a tray of raw barbecue meat and a
bickering couple. Someone else takes the place of shadows you
thought was his.

There is a view of a bare rooftop garden up above, then an exodus
of headlights from the vehicles snaking through the damp street
down below.

Inside the room, you dream of missing the sensation of stone
against skull, tender, reverberating in the head. Inside the room,
you dream of missing the nutty aftertaste of sauteed eggplant, or
the equally nutty savor of grassland during dusk. Then, of the
pitch-black quiet.

You wake up, touching yourself in front of the mirror with the
door unlocked. Behind you, the neon billboards outside reach out
to the window. Smoke from the barbecue grill arrives, scratching
the window pane, poking the glass, knocking, knocking.

THE OLDER GAYS FROM THE HOMETOWN SPEAK OF THE GAY BARS THAT ONCE WERE: AN ORAL HISTORY

Navigator, the most famous. Tubbies, above a bakeshop. Bachelor, at the back of a McDonald's. How a favorite stripper is now a favorite barber.

EPILOGUE

It was a year of downpours, a year of Mercury in endless retrograde. Behind you, C.M. Recto Avenue, a concrete terrain of stupor, your past life rescued as gray semitones. **The road goes away from here**. Your birth chart says this is your reversal year of some planetary node, two years before your Saturn return. The tarot card reader on YouTube predicts you will have intense sex this weekend. **Close the blinds and kill the birds.** *Tell me about your hookup*, I might have to ask you, like any friend would be obliged, *was it the Optics professor from your Discord voice channel, the movie geek you met on Telegram, or your equally depressed fuck buddy from Viber?* Except that I never would. I will instead repeat my fading echo against your radio silence, **see the man but not the light**, mirror yours with mine, **proportioned to share their graves**.

Rain had more than once outdistance the **night, unimpeded, fell** in your side of our city. La Niña, end of the southwest monsoon, as the weather bureau insists like some new convert's passion. You bypassed on the quiet, slip through its sieves, a million little drizzles against tarmac, water once thought to make sound. But **your body told me in a dream it's never been afraid of anything**. So the brutal torrent freefalls on the road leading to Bukidnon, careening upwards like the vein above your collarbone, color of the earthborn, when you're trying to make a point, or those in your right forearm, highlighting the asphalt's onyx. **I shovel the color into our faces, I shovel our faces into our faces**. I must forewarn you that this Lunar Eclipse in your Moon sign will be unsettling. I should caution you about the Gemini in your astrological house of karma and endings. **I tell you these things** ~~because I love you.~~

Townspeople went about bumping their heads in sleep. The queues hose outside Gaisano Mall and the bus stop after Cugman River, a new day, another false tenet, another vain tempo **away from darkness to see daylight, to see what would happen.** How dare I, laureate of loss, reckoned I left gaping holes: **we know this.** How dare I, ruminant of ruins, confuse distance with oblivion: **we know this.** Elsewhere, at the very end of Sayre highway, in a car of a Tinder date whose name resembles yours—**so what's there to be faithful to?**—I renegotiate myself as thoroughfare, scavenger of restraint, bailiwick of delirium. **Today is Sunday.** This landscape alters into a lurid haunt. **The town is empty.**

Your lean torso, a hemisphere on its own, blurs the dusk into phone screen into daybreak into panorama. Everything I see, this urban imaginary, empties into grass blades running the length of road cracks, or an egg shell white wall of a motel, once a quarantine facility, **stake your claim before something smears up the paint**. In the looming darkness, what remains of sundown, like reeds flitting their way through the crevices of the flyover above, through the gaps of its railings below, **the field is empty, sloshed with gold**. *Has it been told that what's long gone could still linger? Isn't grief an inordinate response to loss?* **Yes and yes, the same answers**, dear poet. We are **things that shouldn't touch**. And so, I leave no trail, not even **footprints in the slush of ourselves**, like mist. Tonight, you marvel at the street lights as you pass them by, heading east, hoisted to the safety of home. Tonight, I seek the shade of alleyways, dissolve into the wreckage of this nightfall.

Lines in bold are taken from Richard Siken's *War of the Foxes* (2015).

ACKNOWLEDGEMENTS

I wish to thank the editors of the following anthologies, journals, and magazines where the pieces in this collection were first published in their earlier versions:

Richard Porter of *Now I Know, Daylight: Responses to Untitled No. 1 (1981) by Agnes Martin* (London, England: Pilot Press, 2021): "Portrait of M as Daylight".

Haley Jenkins of *Selcouth Station Press* (London, England): "from The Book of Etiquette for F*ck Buddies".

Brina Patel of *Rituals: An Anthology of Nonfiction and Poetry Exploring the Presence and Significance of Rituals* (Vancouver, Canada: Bell Press Books): "Questions".

Masande Ntshanga and Siphokazi Jonas of *New Contrast Literary Journal* (Claremont, South Africa): "M of the Southern Downpours".

Apiana Den Bleyker of *I <3 the Aughties: Anthology of Writings about the 2000s* (New York, NY: ELJ Editions): "An Anime, A War, and A Dance: Gay Boyhood in Three Sanbunshi".

David Acosta and Susan DiPronio of *Wicked Gay Ways* (Philadelphia, United States): "Car Fun of Hand Jobs Past".

Min Bui Jones of *Mekong Review* (New South Wales, Australia): "D'morvie Suites," "Kathryn Bakeshop," and "Terrazzo Bar".

Acacia Caven and Marije Klei of *Expanded Field Journal* (Amsterdam, The Netherlands): "Cy" (published as "from 'M of the Southern Downpours'").

Noah Ross of *bæst: a journal of queer affects and forms* (California, USA): "Portraits of M in a Milking Video" (published as "from 'M of the Southern Downpours'").

Therese Estacion and Chris Johnson of *Arc Poetry Magazine* (Vancouver, Canada): "V, the Second," "Ivan," and "Jeremy".

Joshua Escobar of *Open Fruit Magazine* (Santa Barbara, California): "Epilogue".

www.ingramcontent.com/pod-product-compliance
Lightning Source LLC
Chambersburg PA
CBHW031753200726
48289CB00013B/930